OLIVER TWIST

Charles Dickens

Among other public buildings in a certain town there is a workhouse, and in this workhouse was born Oliver Twist.

For a long time it remained a matter of doubt whether the child would survive to bear any name at all. Oliver and Nature fought out the point between them. The result was, that after a few struggles, Oliver breathed, sneezed and set up as loud a cry as could reasonably have been expected.

If he could have known he was to be left to the tender mercies of churchwardens and overseers, perhaps he would have cried the louder.

As Oliver gave this first proof of the proper action of his lungs, the pale face of a young woman was raised feebly from the pillow.

Let me see the child and die.

You must not talk about dying yet.

The patient stretched out her hand toward the child. The surgeon deposited it in her arms. She imprinted her cold white lips passionately on its forehead.

Then she gazed wildly round, shuddered, fell back--and died.

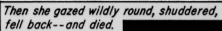

It's all over, Mrs. Thingummy. Where did she come from?

She was found lying in the street. Where she came from, or where she was going to, nobody knows.

The medical gentleman walked away to dinner. The nurse sat down on a low chair before the fire and proceeded to dress the infant. Now that he was enveloped in the old calico robes, he fell into his place at once-- the orphan of a parish workhouse, despised by all, pitied by none.

In time, Oliver was dispatched to a branch workhouse some three miles off, where twenty or thirty other juvenile offenders against the poor laws rolled about the floor all day.

Mrs. Mann was given a sum per small head per week for food. She appropriated the greater part of the weekly stipend to her own use.

Susan, another brat! His name is Oliver. If he bawls too loud, pinch him.

Yes, Mrs. Mann.

Thus, Oliver Twist's ninth birthday found him a pale, thin child, somewhat diminutive in stature and decidedly small in circumference.

One day, Mrs. Mann was unexpectedly startled by the sight of Mr. Bumble, the beadle*, striving to undo the wicket of the garden gate.

Gracious! Is that you, Mr. Bumble, sir?

*a minor parish official

Mrs. Mann ushered the beadle into a small parlour, placed a seat for him and deposited his cocked hat and cane on the table before him.

The child Oliver Twist is nine years old today.

Bless him!

We have never been able to discover who is his father, or what was his mother's settlement, name or condition.

How comes he to have any name at all, then?

I invented it. We name our foundlings in alphabetical order. The last was an S--Swubble, I named him. This was a T--Twist, I named him. I have got names ready-made to the end of the alphabet, and all the way through it again.

Why, you're quite a literary character, sir!

Well, well, perhaps I may be. Oliver being now too old to remain here, the board has determined to have him back into the workhouse. I have come out myself to take him there.

I'll fetch him directly.

Oliver was led away by Mr. Bumble. At the workhouse, he was conducted into a large, whitewashed room, where eight or ten fat gentlemen were sitting round a table.

You have come here to be educated and taught a useful trade.

You'll begin to pick oakum tomorrow morning at six o'clock.

For three months, Oliver Twist, along with his companions, suffered the tortures of slow starvation.

Unless I have another basin of gruel each day, I'm afraid I may some night happen to eat the boy who sleeps next to me.

A council was held. Lots were cast who should walk up to the master after supper that evening and ask for more.

It's fallen to you, Oliver!

The evening arrived. The boys took their places. The master, in his cook's uniform, stationed himself at the copper. The gruel was served out.

The gruel disappeared. The boys whispered to each other and winked at Oliver, while his neighbours nudged him. He rose from the table and advanced to the master, basin and spoon in hand.

Please, sir. I want some more.

The master gazed in stupefied astonishment on the small rebel for some seconds.

What!

Please, sir. I want some more.

The master aimed a blow at Oliver's head with the ladle.

Oliver was ordered into instant confinement. A bill was next morning pasted on the outside of the gate, offering a reward of five pounds to anybody who would take Oliver Twist off the hands of the parish.

You don't know anybody who wants a boy, do you? Liberal terms, Mr. Sowerberry, liberal terms!

I think I'll take the boy myself.

5£   5£
Reward

Mr. Sowerberry was the undertaker. That evening, Oliver was led away to the under-taker's. Here, Mrs. Sowerberry opened a side door and pushed Oliver down a steep flight of stairs into a stone kitchen.

Charlotte, give this boy some of the cold bits that were put by for the dog.

After he had eaten, Oliver was led upstairs to sleep in the shop among the coffins. The recess beneath the counter in which his mattress was thrust looked like a grave.

Oliver was awakened in the morning by a loud kicking at the outside of the shop door. He undid the chain and turned the key.

I beg your pardon, sir. Did you knock?

I kicked. I'm Mister Noah Claypole, and you're under me. Take down the shutters!

In the course of a few weeks, Oliver acquired a great deal of experience. Many were the mournful processions which he headed.

One day, when Oliver and Noah had descended into the kitchen at the usual dinner hour to banquet upon a small joint of mutton, Noah got rather personal.

Your mother was a regular right-down bad one. It's a great deal better that she died when she did, or else she'd have been hung.

Crimson with fury, Oliver started up, overthrew the chair and table and seized Noah by the throat.

Oliver shook him till his teeth chattered, and, in one heavy blow, felled him to the ground.

He'll murder me! Charlotte! Missus! Help! Oliver's gone mad!

Charlotte and Mrs. Sowerberry rushed into the kitchen. They seized and beat Oliver while Noah pummelled him from behind.

Then they dragged him, struggling and shouting, into the dust cellar, and there locked him up.

For the rest of the day, Oliver was shut up. At night, Mrs. Sowerberry ordered him to his dismal bed. But with the first ray of light that struggled through the crevices in the shutters, Oliver arose and unbarred the door. One timid look around, and he was in the open street.

By eight o'clock, he was nearly five miles away from the town. He sat down to rest by the side of a milestone.

LONDON 70

Early on the seventh morning after he had left his native place, Oliver sat, with bleeding feet and covered with dust, upon a door-step. A boy walked up.

Hullo, my covey. What's the matter?

I am very hungry and tired. I have walked a long way. I have been walking these seven days.

Assisting Oliver to rise, the young gentleman took him to a public house. There, Oliver, at his new friend's bidding, made a long and hearty meal.

My name's Jack Dawkins, but my best friends know me as the Artful Dodger. I've got to be in London tonight. I know a respectable old gentleman who will give you lodgings for nothing.

This unexpected offer of shelter was too tempting to be resisted. It was nearly eleven o'clock when they reached London. At last, the Dodger pushed open the door of a house and drew Oliver into the passage.

Here we are, my covey.

Oliver ascended, with much difficulty, the dark and broken stairs. The Dodger threw open the door of a back room and drew Oliver in after him.

Fagin, this is my friend, Oliver Twist.

We are very glad to see you, Oliver, very.

They had supper. Oliver ate his share, and Fagin then mixed him a glass of hot gin-and-water. Immediately afterward, Oliver felt himself gently lifted on to one of the sacks. He sank into a deep sleep.

It was late next morning when Oliver awoke. There was no other person in the room but Fagin. Oliver had scarcely washed himself when the Dodger returned with a sprightly young friend, Charley Bates.

Well, I hope you've been at work this morning, my dears. What have you got?

A couple of pocketbooks. Charley has four hand-kerchiefs.

You'd like to be able to make handker-chiefs as easy as Charley Bates, wouldn't you, my dear?

Very much, indeed, if you'll teach me, sir.

When the breakfast was cleared away, the merry old gentleman and the two boys played at a very curious game. Fagin placed a snuff-box, notecase and a watch in his pockets, and stuck a mock diamond pin in his shirt. Then he trotted up and down the room with a stick. The two boys followed him closely about.

At last, the Dodger trod upon his toes while Charley stumbled up against him. In one moment they took from him the watch, the notecase, the snuffbox, and the pin.

Charley, my dear, I felt your hand in my waist-coat pocket. We must begin the game all over again.

After the game had been played a great many times, the Dodger and Charley went away together. Fagin turned to Oliver.

My handkerchief is hanging out of my pocket. See if you can take it out without my feeling it.

Yes, sir.

Oliver held up the bottom of the pocket with one hand, as he had seen the Dodger hold it, and drew the handkerchief lightly out of it with the other.

Here it is, sir.

You're a clever boy, my dear.

One morning, Fagin placed Oliver under the joint guardianship of Charley and the Dodger. The three boys sallied out. They were just emerging from a narrow court when the Dodger made a sudden stop.

Do you see that old gent at the bookstall? He'll do.

A prime plant.

The two boys walked stealthily across the road and slunk close behind the old gentleman. Oliver walked a few paces after them, looking on in silent amazement.

Suddenly, the Dodger plunged his hand into the old gentleman's pocket and drew out a handkerchief. He handed it to Charley, and both boys ran around the corner at high speed.

Confused and frightened, Oliver took to his heels.

Stop thief!

The cry was taken up by a hundred voices.

Stop thief!

The crowd accumulated at every turning.

Stop thief!

A great lubberly fellow gained upon Oliver and, with a clever blow, stopped him.

The crowd eagerly gathered around.

Is this the boy, sir?

Yes, I am afraid it is the boy.

A police officer at that moment made his way through the crowd and seized Oliver by the collar.

It wasn't me, sir. It was two other boys. They are here somewhere.

Will you stand upon your legs, you young devil?

Oliver, who could hardly stand, made a shift to raise himself on his feet, and was at once lugged along the streets by the collar at a rapid pace.

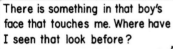
Don't hurt him.

Oliver was led beneath a low archway and up a dirty court to the police office.

I am not sure that this boy actually took the handkerchief. I--I would rather not press the case.

Must go before the magistrate now, sir. His worship will be disengaged in half a minute.

There is something in that boy's face that touches me. Where have I seen that look before?

The old gentleman was roused by a touch on the shoulder. He was at once ushered into the imposing presence of Mr. Fang, the magistrate, who looked up with an angry scowl.

Who are you?

My name, sir, is Brownlow. I had run after the boy because I saw him running away. I do not believe he is actually the thief. I really fear that he is ill.

Mr. Fang sneered.

Come, none of your tricks here, you young vagabond. They won't do. What's your name?

Oliver raised his head and, looking round with imploring eyes, fell to the floor in a fainting fit.

Let him lie there. He'll soon be tired of that. He stands committed for three months--hard labour, of course. Clear the office.

A couple of men were preparing to carry the insensible boy to his cell, when an elderly man rushed hastily into the office and advanced toward the bench.

Stop! The robbery was committed by another boy. I saw it done. I keep the bookstall.

Oliver was discharged and carried out in the yard. Mr. Brownlow found him lying on his back, his shirt unbuttoned, his face a deadly white.

Poor boy, poor boy! Call a coach, somebody, pray. Directly!

A coach was obtained, and Oliver was laid carefully on the seat. The coach rattled away. It stopped before a neat house. Here, a bed was prepared in which Mr. Brownlow saw his young charge carefully deposited.

For many days, Oliver remained insensible to all the goodness of his new friends. He awoke at last from what seemed to have been a long and troubled dream.

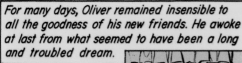

Where have I been brought to?

Hush, my dear. You must be very quiet, or you will be ill again. I am Mrs. Bedwin, the housekeeper.

In three days' time, he was able to sit in an easy chair, well propped up with pillows. Mrs. Bedwin had him carried downstairs into her room.

The doctor says Mr. Brownlow may come in to see you this morning.

Oliver fixed his eyes most intently on a portrait which hung against the wall just opposite his chair.

What a beautiful, mild face that lady's is. It makes my heart beat as if the portrait were alive and wanted to speak to me, but couldn't.

There came a soft rap at the door, and in walked Mr. Brownlow.

How do you feel, my dear?

Very happy, sir, and very grateful indeed, sir, for your goodness to me.

The old gentleman looked steadily on Oliver's face. The resemblance between Oliver's features and some familiar face came upon him so strongly that he could not withdraw his gaze. He pointed to the picture over Oliver's head and then to the boy's face. Every feature was the same.

One evening, about a week after the affair of the picture, Mr. Brownlow called Oliver to his study.

Let me hear your story, my dear, where you come from, who brought you up, and how you got into the company in which I found you. Speak the truth, and you shall not be friendless while I live.

When Oliver was on the point of beginning, a peculiarly impatient double knock was heard at the street door, and the servant announced Mr. Grimwig.

He is an old friend of mine, Oliver. Do not mind his rough manners. He is a worthy creature at bottom.

At this moment, there walked into the room, supporting himself by a thick stick, a stout old gentleman.

So that's the boy who had the fever, is it? How are you, boy?

A great deal better, thank you, sir.

Mr. Grimwig removed his gloves, sat down and, opening a double eyeglass, took a view of Oliver.

And when are you going to hear a full, true and particular account of the life and adventures of Oliver Twist?

Tomorrow morning. I would rather he was alone with me at the time.

Mr. Grimwig whispered to Mr. Brownlow.

I'll tell you what. He is deceiving you, my good friend.

I'll swear he is not.

As fate would have it, Mrs. Bedwin chanced to bring in at this moment a small parcel of books, which Mr. Brownlow had purchased that morning.

Stop the delivery boy, Mrs. Bedwin. There is something to go back.

He has gone, sir.

Dear me, I am very sorry for that. I particularly wished those books to be returned tonight.

Send Oliver with them. He will be sure to deliver them safely, you know.

The old gentleman was just going to say that Oliver should not go out on any account, when a most malicious cough from Mr. Grimwig determined him that he should.

You shall go, my dear. You are to say that you have brought those books back, and that you have come to pay the four pound ten I owe him. This is a five-pound note, so you will have to bring me back ten shillings change.

Oliver departed. Mr. Brownlow pulled out his watch and placed it on the table.

Let me see. He'll be back in twenty minutes.

The boy has a new suit of clothes on his back, a set of valuable books under his arm and a five-pound note in his pocket. He'll join his old friends, the thieves, and laugh at you. If ever that boy returns to this house, sir, I'll eat my head.

On his way to the book-stall, Oliver accidentally turned down a by-street.

He was walking along, thinking how happy and contented he ought to feel, when he was stopped by a pair of arms thrown tight around his neck.

Oh, my dear brother! Thank gracious goodness heavens, I've found him.

Let go of me. Who is it? What are you stopping me for?

A man burst out of a beer shop, with a white dog at his heels, and seized Oliver.

Come home to your poor mother, you young dog! Come home directly.

Go home, you little brute.

In another moment, he was dragged into a labyrinth of dark narrow courts and was forced along them at a pace which rendered the few cries he dared to give utterance to unintelligible.

At length, they turned into a very filthy, narrow street and stopped before a house that was in a ruinous condition. The man seized the terrified boy by the collar, and all three were quickly inside the house.

Is the old one here?

Yes, and precious down in the mouth he has been. Won't he be glad to see Oliver!

They crossed an empty kitchen and, opening the door of a low, earthy-smelling room, were received with a shout of laughter.

Delighted to see you looking so well, my dear. Why didn't you write, my dear, and say you were coming?

Fagin seized the five-pound note.

Hallo, what's that? If that ain't mine and Nancy's, I'll take the boy back again.

Mine, Bill Sikes! You shall have the books.

But Sikes plucked the note from between Fagin's finger and thumb, folded it up small and tied it in his neckerchief.

That's for our share of the trouble and not half enough, neither. You may keep the books, if you're fond of reading. If you ain't, sell them.

Oliver fell upon his knees at Fagin's feet, in perfect desperation.

They belong to the good, kind, old gentleman who took me into his house. Keep me here all my life long, but pray, send him back the books and money. He'll think I stole them.

Oliver, you're right. He will think you have stolen them. It couldn't have happened better.

Oliver jumped suddenly to his feet and tore wildly from the room, uttering shrieks for help. Fagin and his two pupils darted out in pursuit.

Keep back the dog, Bill! He'll tear the boy to pieces!

The Dodger and Charley Bates returned, dragging Oliver between them. Fagin took up a jagged and knotted club which lay in a corner of the fireplace and inflicted a smart blow on Oliver's shoulders. Nancy wrested the club from his hands.

You've got the boy, and what more would you have? Let him be.

Then Master Bates led Oliver into an adjacent kitchen and produced the identical old suit of clothes which Oliver had left off at Mr. Brownlow's.

Thought you got rid of these, did you? The housekeeper didn't know she sold them to a friend of ours. Now put off the smart ones.

Master Bates rolled up the new clothes under his arm, and locked the door behind him. And so Oliver remained for many days, seeing nobody, between early morning and midnight, and left during the long hours to commune with his own thoughts.

After the lapse of a week or so, Oliver was at liberty to wander about the house. One evening...

I have come from Bill. You are to go with me.

Outside, a hackney was in waiting. Nancy pulled Oliver in with her. The driver lashed his horse into full speed.

At last, the carriage stopped. A moment later, Oliver and Nancy were in a house.

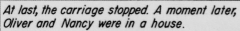

So you've got the kid. Did he come quiet?

Like a lamb.

Sikes pulled off Oliver's cap and threw it into a corner. He sat himself down by the table, stood the boy in front of him and took up a pocket pistol which lay on the table.

Do you know what this is?

Yes, sir.

The robber grasped Oliver's wrist and put the barrel close to his temple.

Well, if you speak a word when you're out-of-doors with me, except when I speak to you, the loading will be in your head without notice.

It was a cheerless morning when they got into the street. Oliver kept up with the rapid strides of Sikes as well as he could.

Come, don't lag behind already, lazylegs!

At nightfall, they stood before a solitary house, all ruinous and decayed, some miles from London. The door yielded to pressure, and Sikes and Oliver passed in together.

Bill, my boy! I'm glad to see you. I was almost afraid you'd given it up.

Toby, this is one of Fagin's lads. Oliver, sit down by the fire and rest yourself. You'll have to go out with Toby and me tonight.

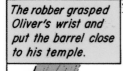

After some food, Oliver fell into a heavy doze. He was roused by Toby Crackit.

It's half-past one!

Sikes fastened on Oliver's cape, then the two robbers issued forth with the boy between them. It was now intensely dark.

After walking about a quarter of a mile, they stopped before a house surrounded by a wall. Toby Crackit climbed to the top in a twinkling.

The boy next. Hoist him up. I'll catch hold of him.

Soon, all were on the other side. They stole cautiously toward the house. For the first time, Oliver saw that robbery, if not murder, was the object of the expedition. He sank upon his knees.

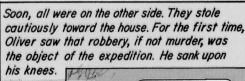

For God's sake, let me go! Do not make me steal.

Get up! Get up, or I'll strew your brains upon the grass.

Toby placed his hand upon the boy's mouth and dragged him to the house.

Say another word, and you'll get a crack on the head. Bill, wrench the shutter open.

Sikes applied a crowbar vigorously, but with little noise. After some delay, the shutter swung open on its hinges. He then drew a dark lantern from his pocket and threw the glare full on Oliver's face.

Now listen, you young limb. I'm going to put you through there. Take this light. Go softly along the hall to the street door. Unfasten it and let us in.

Sikes put Oliver gently through the window and planted him safely on the floor inside. Oliver had resolved he would make one effort to alarm the family. He started for some stairs.

Come back!

Scared by the sudden breaking of the dead stillness, and by a loud cry which followed it, Oliver let his lantern fall.

The cry was repeated--a light appeared-- a vision of two terrified, half-dressed men at the top of the stairs swam before his eyes-- a flash--a loud noise--and he staggered back.

Sikes had him by the collar and dragged him through the window. Oliver had the sensation of being carried over uneven ground at a rapid pace.

They've hit him. How the boy bleeds!

It's all up, Bill! Drop the kid, and show them your heels.

Sikes threw the prostrate form of Oliver in a dry ditch. The boy lay motionless and insensible.

The air grew colder, as day came slowly on. With a low cry of pain, the boy awoke.

Oliver got upon his feet and essayed to walk. His head was dizzy, and he staggered to and fro, stumbling toward the house. There, he knocked faintly at the door, then sunk down against one of the pillars.

A boy!

The servant seized the boy by one leg and arm and lugged him into a hall. He deposited him at full length on the floor.

Here's one of the thieves, Miss Rose! Wounded, Miss!

Bring the poor creature upstairs and put him in your room.

Oliver was placed in bed. Soon, a doctor came and bound his wounded arm. Then the boy fell in a deep sleep.

Rose, this poor child can never have been the pupil of robbers.

Even if he has been wicked, dear aunt, think how young he is. He may never have known a mother's love. Don't let them drag this sick child to a prison.

On the night Oliver was wounded, Mrs. Thingummy, who had helped bring the boy into the world, was drawing her last breath. Mrs. Corney, the workhouse matron, bent over her.

Listen to me. I must tell you. In this very room, I once nursed a pretty creature. She gave birth to to a boy and died.

I robbed her, so I did! I stole it -- rich gold that might have saved her life!

Gold! Who was the mother? When was it?

Mrs. Thingummy groaned.

She charged me to keep it safe. But I stole it in my heart when she first showed it to me hanging round her neck. They would have treated the boy better, if they had known it all.

The boy's name!

They called him Oliver. The gold I stole was--

Yes, yes-- what?

But Mrs. Thingummy had fallen lifeless on the bed. Slowly, Mrs. Corney opened the dead woman's hand. In it was a pawnbroker's ticket.

While these things were passing in the country work-house, Fagin was brooding over a dull, smoky fire. Toby Crackit entered.

The crack failed. They fired and hit the boy. Bill and I parted company and left the youngster lying in a ditch.

Fagin stopped to hear no more. He rushed from the house to where Sikes lived.

If Sikes comes back and leaves the boy behind him, murder him yourself if you would have him escape the gallows. The boy's worth hundreds of pounds to me!

Fagin again turned his face homeward. He had reached the corner of his own street, and was already fumbling in his pocket for the doorkey, when a dark figure glided up to him.

Fagin! Where the devil have you been?

On your business, my dear. On your business all night.

They entered the house. For a quarter of an hour they talked in a small room.

Why didn't you make a snivelling pickpocket of Oliver at once? Couldn't you have gotten him convicted, and sent him safely out of the kingdom?

My dear Monks, it was not easy to train him to the business. He was not like other boys in the same circumstances.

Suddenly, Monks started.

I saw the shadow of a woman pass along like a breath!

Meanwhile, Oliver gradually throve and prospered under the united care of Rose and Mrs. Maylie. He told them the story of his life.

If Mr. Brownlow and Mrs. Bedwin knew how happy I am, they would be pleased, I am sure.

When you are well enough to bear the journey, we will send you to see them.

In a short time, Oliver was sufficiently recovered to undergo the expedition. One morning, he and Mr. Losberne, a surgeon, set out in a little carriage. When the coach turned into the street where Mr. Brownlow resided, Oliver's heart beat violently.

Now, my boy, which house is it?

That house! The white house!

But the white house was empty.

We'll knock at the next door.

At the adjoining house, a servant answered Mr. Losberne's knock.

What has become of Mr. Brownlow, do you know?

Mr. Brownlow, sir? He sold his goods and has gone to the West Indies. He, the housekeeper and a friend all went together.

Mr. Losberne led Oliver to the carriage.

My poor boy, we will go home.

Spring flew swiftly by, and summer came. One beautiful night, Rose sat down to the piano. She fell into a low and very solemn air.

My dear child, what distresses you? I never saw you so before.

Close the window, pray! I fear I am ill, aunt.

When morning came, Rose was in the first stage of a dangerous fever.

Oliver, this letter must be sent to Mr. Losberne. It must be carried to the inn in the market-town and dispatched by horseback.

Oliver ran to the inn at the greatest speed he could muster. The little parcel was handed up, and the man set spurs to his horse.

Oliver was turning out of the gateway when he accidentally stumbled against a tall man. The man shook his fist.

Death! Rot you! What are you doing here?

Oliver darted away. The circumstance did not dwell in his recollection long. The next day, late at night, Mr. Losberne arrived.

She is so young, so much beloved, but there is very little hope.

Another day passed. Mrs. Maylie and Oliver sat, afraid to speak, for hours. Then their ears caught the sound of a footstep.

Tell me, in the name of heaven! Is she dying?

No. As He is good and merciful, she will live to bless us all, for years to come.

That night, Mrs. Maylie's son Harry arrived.

If Rose's illness had ended differently, Mother, how could I ever have known happiness again!

Now the days were flying by. Each morning, Oliver and Harry gathered flowers for Rose's chamber.

One evening, Oliver sat at a window, intent upon his books. By slow degrees, he fell asleep.

Suddenly, there -- at the window -- close before Oliver -- with his eyes peering into the room, stood Fagin! And beside him were the scowling features of the very man who had accosted Oliver in the inn yard.

It is he, sure enough.

He! Could I mistake him?

It was but an instant, a glance, a flash before Oliver's eyes, and they were gone. Oliver stood transfixed for a moment. Then, leaping from the window into the garden, he called loudly for help.

Fagin! It is Fagin!

What direction did he take?

That.

The search was all in vain.

It must have been a dream, Oliver.

No, indeed, sir. I saw them both, as plainly as I see you now.

After a few days, the affair began to be forgotten. Meanwhile, Rose was rapidly recovering. One morning, when she was alone in the breakfast-parlour, Harry Maylie entered.

Rose, such a rushing torrent of fears I had lest you should die, and never know how devotedly I loved you.

You must endeavour to forget me as the object of your love.

From your own lips, let me hear why you won't have me for your husband.

The prospect before you is a brilliant one. Your mother adopted me. A nameless orphan cannot be the wife of a man who seeks a career in public life.

While the events that had befallen Oliver occurred, Mr. Bumble had married Mrs. Corney, the workhouse matron.

You going to sit snoring there, all day? Get up and take yourself away from here.

I'm going, my dear.

Mr. Bumble slunk away. He walked up one street and down another. At length, he paused before a public house, then entered.

Gin-and-water.

He drank in silence and found that the man at the next table was looking at him.

I have seen you before, I think. You were beadle here, once, were you not?

I was, young man. Now I am master of the workhouse.

The other man pushed a couple of sovereigns to Mr. Bumble.

I want some information from you--about a pale-faced boy who was apprenticed to a coffinmaker, and the hag that nursed his mother.

Why, you mean young Twist! As for the nurse, she died last winter. My wife was with her when she died.

Bumble's companion produced a scrap of paper and wrote an obscure address on it. Then he told Bumble to bring his wife to him at nine the next evening.

It will be done, sir. What name am I to ask for?

Monks.

The next evening, Mr. and Mrs. Bumble directed their course toward a colony of ruinous houses bordering upon the river. Soon, they were inside one of the houses and seated at a table with Monks.

The sooner we come to our business, the better for all. You were with the hag the night she died. Did she tell you anything about the mother of this Oliver Twist?

Give me five-and-twenty pounds in gold, and I'll tell you all I know.

Monks thrust his hand into a side pocket. Producing a canvas bag, he told out twenty-five sovereigns on the table and pushed them over to the woman.

She spoke of a young creature who had brought this Oliver into the world some years before, and said that she had robbed her. Without saying more, she fell back and died. In her hand, I found a pawnbroker's duplicate. I redeemed the pledge.

She threw upon the table a small kid bag, which Monks tore open with trembling hands. It contained a little gold locket and a plain, gold wedding ring.

That's what I got. The locket has the name Agnes engraved on the inside.

Monks suddenly wheeled the table aside and threw back a large trap door. Water was rushing below, and into it he threw the locket and ring.

If the sea ever gives up its dead, it will keep its gold and silver and that trash among it.

On the evening following that upon which the three worthies disposed of their little matter of business, Mr. William Sikes awakened with a fever. He sent Nancy to Fagin's for money.

I'll get you the cash, Nancy.

The murmur of a man's voice reached her ears. Fagin carried a candle to the door, as a man's step was heard upon the stairs without. It was Monks.

Any news?

Let me have a word with you.

Monks and Fagin went upstairs. Before the sound of their footsteps had ceased to echo through the house, the girl had slipped off her shoes, glided from the room, ascended the stairs, and listened at the door.

A quarter of an hour later, the girl glided back. Immediately afterward, the two men were heard descending. When Fagin returned, the girl was adjusting her shawl and bonnet.

Come, give me the money and let me get back to Bill.

She soon reached the dwelling where she had left the housebreaker. Sikes called for his medicine. Several minutes after he had drunk it, Sikes fell into a deep and heavy sleep, and Nancy hurried from the house.

Nancy rushed along the streets. At last, she reached a family hotel in a quiet but handsome street.

Now, young woman! Who do you want here?

A lady who is stopping in this house-- Miss Maylie.

A little while later, Nancy and Rose Maylie were seated in a small antechamber.

Do you know a man named Monks? He knows you, and knew you were here.

No--I never heard the name.

Nancy related the conversation she had overheard between Monks and Fagin.

Monks said that the only proofs of the boy's identity lie at the bottom of the river, and he had got Oliver's money safely now, and if he could gratify his hatred by taking the boy's life without bringing his own neck in danger, he would.

Monks said he might harm him yet. His very words were, "In short, Fagin, you never laid such snares as I'll contrive for my young brother, Oliver."

His brother!

Nancy rose to leave.

It is growing late. I have to reach home without suspicion of having been on such an errand as this. Every Sunday night, from eleven to midnight, I will walk on London Bridge if you wish to reach me.

Upon the night when Nancy hurried on her self-imposed mission to Rose Maylie, Noah Claypole and Charlotte entered London. They stopped at an inn.

Give us a bit of cold meat and a drop of beer.

They were ushered into a small back room, and the required viands were set before them. Fagin, in the course of his evening's business, came into the bar.

Hush! Strangers in the next room.

Ah. They may be of interest. I'll have a look and listen.

Mounting a stool, Fagin cautiously applied his eye to a pane of glass.

No more jolly old coffins, Charlotte. In London, there's pockets to be picked and banks to be robbed.

The appearance of a stranger interrupted him.

I have taken a fancy to you and the young woman. Let me have a word with you.

Charlotte, see to them bundles.

When Charlotte left, Fagin clapped Noah on the shoulder.

I have got a friend that I think can put you in the right way. Tomorrow, you and the girl be here.

The next day, Oliver, who had been walking in the streets with the servant Giles for a body-guard, returned to Rose's room in breathless haste.

I have seen Mr. Brownlow getting out of a coach and going into a house! His address is in Craven Street!

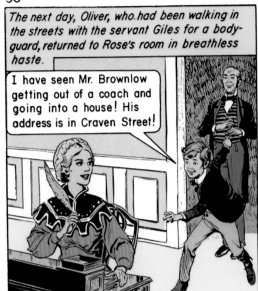

In little more than five minutes, they were on their way to the address. Rose left Oliver in the coach, and went in alone to speak to Mr. Brownlow. The old gentleman hurried outside to see Oliver.

My boy! My boy!

That evening, Oliver's friends held a solemn conference.

We shall have difficulty in getting to the bottom of the mystery about Oliver, unless we can bring this man, Monks, upon his knees. Perhaps Nancy will point out Monks. If not, she may give us a description of his person.

Sunday night came. As Sikes and Fagin were talking, Nancy put on her bonnet and prepared to leave the room.

Where are you going?

I want a breath of air.

Sikes rose, locked the door and took the key out.

Put your head out the window. You're going nowhere.

Next morning, Fagin gave Noah a task.

I want you to spy on one of us -- a young woman named Nancy.

I can do that pretty well, I know. I was a regular sneak in school.

The following Sunday night, Nancy advanced with rapid steps on London Bridge. Behind her, in the deepest shadow he could find, slunk Noah Claypole.

Rose Maylie, accompanied by Mr. Brownlow, alighted from a carriage within a short distance of the bridge. Nancy met them. Then they descended upon some landing stairs by the river.

You were not here last Sunday night.

I couldn't come. I was kept by force.

At Brownlow's query, Nancy described Monks.

You have given us valuable assistance, young woman. What can I do to serve you?

You can do nothing to help me, sir. I am past all hope, indeed.

After they had gone, Noah Claypole crept slowly from his hiding place and made for Fagin's house as fast as his legs would carry him.

Two hours before daybreak, the spy told Fagin and Sikes what he had overheard. Sikes dashed into the silent streets to his own door. He opened it softly and roused Nancy from her sleep.

Bill, why do you look at me like that?

You were watched to-night! Every word you said was heard! Get up!

The robber dragged her into the middle of the room, then seized a heavy club and struck her down.

The day passed, and the twilight was beginning to close in, when Mr. Brownlow alighted from a coach at his own door. With him were two sturdy men and Monks.

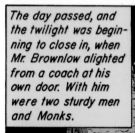

By what authority am I kidnapped in the street and brought here by these men?

By mine.

In the house, Monks and Brownlow were left alone together.

This is pretty treatment, sir, from my father's oldest friend.

It is because I was your father's oldest friend that I am moved to treat you gently now--yes, Edward Leeford, even now.

What is the name to me?

Nothing to you. I am very glad you have changed it. You have a brother, although you have destroyed the proofs of his birth and parentage-- a locket and a ring--so that you would inherit all that your father left!

A few hours after Mr. Brownlow's meeting with Monks, Sikes and his dog came to a small village. A stage-coach, with the mail from London, was standing in the street.

Anything new in the city, Ben?

I heard talk of a murder--a woman was killed. But they'll have the murderer yet.

Sikes plunged into the darkness of the road. Every object before him took on the semblance of some fearful thing. Every breath of wind came laden with Nancy's low cry.

I'll go back to London. They'll never expect to nab me there. I'll lie by for a week or so and, with money from Fagin, get to France.

The next day he arrived in the filthiest, the strangest, the most extraordinary of the many localities that are hidden in London --Jacob's Island.

There, in an upper room of an abandoned, crumbling house, some of Fagin's gang were in secret residence.

Tonight's paper says that Fagin's took. Is it true, or a lie?

True.

Charley Bates entered the room. Looking with horror upon the murderer's face, the boy retreated.

Charley, don't you know me?

Don't come near me. You monster!

Sikes' eyes sunk gradually to the ground.

Witness you three--I'm not afraid of him. If they come here after him, I'll give him up. I'd give him up if he was to be boiled alive.

The boy threw himself upon the strong man, and in the intensity of his energy and the suddenness of his surprise, brought him heavily to the ground.

Murderer! Help! Down with him!

The contest, however, was too unequal to last long. Sikes had the boy down, and his knee was on his throat, when there came a loud knocking at the door, and then a hoarse murmur from a multitude of angry voices.

Help! He's here! Break down the door!

Strokes, thick and heavy, rattled upon the door. The desperate ruffian threw up the window sash and menaced the crowd.

Do your worst! I'll cheat you yet!

Twenty guineas to the man who brings a ladder!

The murderer staggered back into the room and shut the faces out.

The tide was in as I came up. Give me a long rope. They're all in front. I may drop into the ditch in the back and clear off that way.

The panic-stricken men pointed to where such articles were kept. The murderer, hastily selecting the longest and strongest cord, hurried up to the housetop.

The water's out. The ditch is a bed of mud!

Sikes determined to make one last effort for his life by dropping into the ditch. He set his foot against the stack of chimneys, fastened one end of the rope firmly round it, and with the other made a strong, running noose.

At the very instant when he brought the loop over his head previous to slipping it beneath his armpits, the murderer threw his arms above his head and uttered a yell of terror.

Nancy's eyes are staring at me!

He lost his balance and tumbled over the parapet.

There was a sudden jerk, and he swung lifeless against the wall. His dog ran forward on the parapet with a dismal howl. He jumped for the dead man's shoulders. Missing his aim, he struck his head against a stone and died.

The events of Sikes' death were yet but two days old, when Oliver found himself in an inn of his native town with Rose and Mrs. Maylie. The door opened, and Mr. Losberne and Mr. Grimwig entered, followed by Mr. Brownlow and Monks.

This child is your half-brother, the son of your father, my dear friend, Edwin Leeford, by poor young Agnes Fleming, who died giving him birth.

Yes. That is their son.

Your father made an unhappy marriage and early separated from his wife. One day he brought me a portrait of a girl whom he said he dearly loved. He hinted he would soon leave England with her, for she was about to bear his child.

Monks scowled at the trembling boy.

But he died soon after. In his desk, my mother found a will, leaving her and me a small sum.

The bulk of the property he divided into two equal portions--one for Agnes Fleming, and the other for their child, if it should be born alive and ever come of age.

If the child were a girl, it was to inherit the money unconditionally. But if a boy, only on the stipulation that in his minority he should never have stained his name with any public act of dishonour, meanness, cowardice or wrong.

He did this, he said, to mark his confidence in the mother, and his conviction that the child would share her gentle heart.

When my mother lay upon her death bed, I swore to her, if ever the child crossed my path, that I would spit upon that insulting will by dragging the child to the very gallows-foot, if it were a boy.

Oliver came in this man's way at last, and he gave Fagin a large reward for keeping Oliver ensnared.

There are only a few remaining words to say. The father of the unhappy Agnes had two daughters. Monks, what was the fate of the other -- the child?

Agnes' father retreated with his children into a remote corner of Wales. One night, Agnes left her home in secret. The father searched for her on foot in every town and village near.

Agnes' father died in a strange place, after seeking her in vain. The other child, Agnes' sister, was taken in by some wretched cottagers, who reared it as their own. My mother found the child, but left it with them until a widow lady saw the girl by chance and took her home.

Mrs. Maylie folded Rose in her arms.

My sweet companion, my own dear girl!

Oliver threw his arms around Rose's neck.

Not aunt. I'll never call her aunt--sister, my own dear sister! Rose, dear, darling Rose!

The others stole from the room. Rose and Oliver were a long time alone. A soft tap at the door at length announced that someone was without. Oliver opened it, glided away and gave place to Harry Maylie.

Dear Rose, I know it all.

There are smiling fields and waving trees in England's richest country, and by one village church--mine, Rose, my own!-- there stands a rustic dwelling which you can make me prouder of than all the hopes I have renounced.

Before three months had passed, Rose and Harry Maylie were married in the village church, which was henceforth to be the scene of the young clergyman's labours. Mrs. Maylie took up her abode with her son and daughter-in-law.

Fagin was tried for his crimes and sentenced to be hanged.

Monks retired to a distant part of the New World, where he once more fell into his old courses and, at length, died in prison.

Mr. Brownlow adopted Oliver as his son, and moved with him and the old housekeeper to within a mile of the parsonage. Oliver is visited by Mr. Grimwig a great many times in the course of the year.

And within the altar of the old village church there stands a white marble tablet, which bears as yet but one word --Agnes. May it be many, many years before another name is placed above it.

The End

Charles Dickens

WHEN Charles Dickens was a child, he would accompany his father on walks along the English countryside. Once they passed a beautiful house at the top of Gad's Hill in Kent. The boy told his father that he liked it. His father replied that if he worked very hard, he might someday be able to live in it.

Charles Dickens was a poor boy, and it was his dream to one day live in that big house. He had been born in 1812, the second in a family of eight children. His father, John Dickens, was a clerk who never seemed to have enough money to support his family. They drifted from one shabby home to another.

John Dickens' money troubles finally caused him to be sent to debtor's prison. He took his wife and youngest children with him. In those days, prisons provided family quarters.

Charles Dickens, who was twelve at the time, lived in a garret and got a job in a blacking warehouse. He worked twelve hours a day, six days a week, putting labels on bottles of blacking. On Sundays, he visited his family in prison.

After three months of this, his family received an unexpected grant of money, and his father was able to leave debtor's prison. Charles Dickens happily quit his job and was sent to a private school. He later wrote, "the school was remarkable for white mice and birds. The boys trained the mice much better than the masters trained the boys."

Dickens had to leave the school after two years, when money again became scarce. He taught himself shorthand in order to get a job. In *David Copperfield* he describes the nightmare of dots, circles and "marks like flies' legs" which he suffered in mastering shorthand.

He got a job as a court reporter, and later moved up to the Reporters' Gallery of the House of Commons. But, as he once said, reporting was echoing what other people said, and he wanted to see his own words in print. He sent a short sketch to a publisher, and it was accepted. He was so happy, he later recalled, that he wept with joy and pride.

He began writing more sketches, signing them "Boz," the family nickname for a younger brother. The success of these sketches led to his writing a series of articles called *Pickwick Papers*, which brought him instant fame.

The week that *Pickwick Papers* began their appearance, Dickens married Catherine Hogarth. This was the year 1836, and it marked his step, at the age of twenty-four, into security and success.

Soon Dickens' fame spread to America. In 1842, he and his wife toured America, and were greeted with great excitement and enthusiasm.

Dickens returned to England and continued to write. He remained rich and successful, and was able to fulfill his childhood dream by purchasing the house on Gad's Hill.

He founded a newspaper, a weekly journal and a magazine. Several of his famous books appeared in serial form in his magazine. Many of the articles that he wrote, as well as many of his books, dealt with the social evils of the period. Remembering his own childhood, he fought for reforms in prisons, poorhouses and slums.

Dickens frequently gave public readings from his works. His ability to capture an audience was so great that people sometimes fainted or froze with horror when he read frightening passages.

In 1867, he again toured America. Upon his return to England, the strain of the tour, of writing, public readings, and supporting his family of ten children was too much for him. One evening in 1870, he died while working on a new book.

Themes

Plot and Themes

Oliver Twist is first and foremost a novel of social criticism. Victorian England was a nation of stark contrasts between the rich and the poor and conditions were particularly bad at the time. Poverty and hunger, unemployment, homelessness, disease and crime were major problems. Even people who had jobs suffered: working conditions were unpleasant and unsafe, pay was low, hours were long and child labour was the norm. Dickens wanted to expose the misery and despair of poor people and the injustices and cruelties they faced and he wanted the more privileged classes to face up to the problems and do something about them.

Oliver Twist is also a book that is, in a sense, arguing with itself over the difficult philosophical question of human nature: are people inherently good (or bad), or are they products of their circumstances? The novel doesn't give any clear cut answers. Sometimes it suggests that people are the products of their environment; that poverty and misery are what drive people to crime, rather than any innate moral failing. At other times, the book seems to support a more traditional view that people only make moral choices according to their natures.

The book has often been read as a moral fable, in which good and evil battle it out with Oliver as the battleground. But if we look closer, it's not that simple. Good and evil may at first appear to be clear-cut: Oliver is a good boy, Noah Claypole is a very bad one; Mr Brownlow and the Maylies are kindly, Fagin and Sikes are lowlife villains, and so forth. But there are characters who don't fit so neatly into these categories. The guardians of Oliver's early childhood, Mr Bumble, Mrs Mann, and the Sowerberrys, are "respectable" citizens with the responsibility of caring for the welfare of the poor - who inflict misery and even death on their charges.

In *Oliver Twist* Dickens is specifically targeting the Poor Law Amendment Act of 1834, which was, essentially, welfare reform, and reduced the amount of aid to paupers to discourage them from relying on public assistance. This is why the food rations were so meagre in the workhouse: hunger and discomfort were supposed to drive paupers out to find work. It is in the workhouse that the famous scene occurs in which Oliver dares to ask for more food. The workhouse authorities are outraged by the request, and one board member declares in disgust that Oliver is destined to be hung as a common criminal. The pathos of a hungry child's modest request for more gruel is a comment on the larger issue of the rights of the poor and the working classes to a larger share of the nation's wealth.

Oliver is treated like a criminal by the workhouse board: he's put in solitary confinement and publicly flogged as an example to the other boys. Oliver is apprenticed to the funeral business of Mr and Mrs Sowerberry, where he is abused by Mrs Sowerberry, Noah Claypole and Charlotte. When Oliver can no longer tolerate the abuse, he becomes a homeless runaway, making his way to London, where he meets Jack Dawkins - the Artful Dodger. Dodger is different from anyone Oliver has ever known, and speaks a cockney street slang that Oliver can barely understand. He treats the half-starved Oliver to a "long and hearty meal," and offers him a free place to stay.

Dodger leads Oliver to Fagin's hideout through the mean streets of London. This is the notorious section of London called Saffron Hill, a part of town that Dickens's middle-class readers would not have dared to visit - even the police were reluctant to go there: a dangerous, forbidden place, as the London slums were perceived by the upper classes. London is repeatedly described in the novel as a dark and treacherous maze, with Newgate prison and the hangman's rope at the centre of it all. The city is a powerful presence in the book. Dickens describes it realistically, with many references to actual places, yet *Cont'd* also endows it with a nightmare quality that gives the book a psychological dimension as well. So Oliver is adopted by a gang of criminals who subject him to a new kind of apprenticeship: he's trained to become a pickpocket and burglar.

One of the great ironies of the novel is the question of which group of "guardians" is worse: the cruel and corrupt officials to whom the government entrusts Oliver or the criminals who find him wandering the streets. Both groups abuse and exploit him, yet at times the reader is tempted to prefer the criminals: Fagin's den may be a sinister place, but there's plenty of food and laughter, both of which were in short supply at the workhouse. But then another group of guardians comes into the picture: the respectable members of the upper classes. Wealthy and benevolent, they help Oliver find his rightful place in the world. Mr Brownlow rescues Oliver from the gang the first time, when Oliver is mistakenly arrested for robbing him. Yet Brownlow and Grimwig must then test him with the errand. The test reveals these men's ignorance of real life on the streets: they see Oliver's dilemma as one of moral choice, but for him it's a matter of survival. He promptly falls back into the clutches of Sikes and Nancy, who are waiting for him.

Nancy is another important character who doesn't fit neatly into any moral category. She's a "fallen" woman who would have been considered outcast from respectable society; yet Nancy turns out to be one of the most generous and courageous figures in the book. The strict moral code of the Victorians, with its sexual double standard, condemned women like Nancy and Oliver's mother, Agnes, on moral grounds - yet Dickens portrayed these women sympathetically. He understood that women like Nancy became prostitutes out of economic necessity; they were poor and had few opportunities to earn a decent living. His sympathetic portrayal of these fallen women is an indictment of the hypocrisy and injustice Dickens deplored in his society.

With Oliver back in his clutches, Fagin steps up his efforts to corrupt the boy and sends him on a big house-breaking job with Sikes. Oliver gets another chance to escape when the burglary is botched, and he's left behind at the Maylies' home with a gunshot wound. The scenes of Oliver's life with Mr Brownlow and then with the Maylies are less realistic than those in the criminal underworld. They have the feel of romantic wish-fulfilment: the motherly Mrs Bedwin, the almost magical portrait of Agnes, the beautiful Rose, the idyllic cottage and of course, the outrageous coincidences that have brought Oliver miraculously back into the bosom of his own long-lost family. At the climax of the book the plot shifts again, to focus on the fates of Nancy, Sikes and Fagin. The narrative reverts to a more realistic mode, interspersed with some intensely melodramatic moments.

Fagin makes sure that Sikes finds out about Nancy's efforts to help Oliver, knowing that Sikes will see this as a betrayal, and that he will probably react violently. From what we know about Fagin, it's safe to assume that he wants both Nancy and Sikes dead so that they can never testify against him. Sikes is in a daze after killing Nancy, horrified by the blood and gore and by Nancy's dead eyes staring at him. He flees from the scene and wanders for days in torment, an utter outcast. Eventually he returns to London, and in a bizarre and gruesome scene he is hounded to his death by an angry mob.

Meanwhile, the details of Oliver's happy ending are being worked out: he's adopted by Mr Brownlow and he will inherit money from his father. Harry Maylie gives up his political ambitions so that Rose will consent to marry him but despite this happy ending which Dickens's readers virtually demanded, the book remains a dark description of the times and Dickens's ability to enter into the minds of his criminal characters and his vivid representation of their misery and desperation are an important part of what makes *Oliver Twist* a great book.